# SCOOBY-DOO!
## AND THE
# Rock 'n' Roll
# Zombie

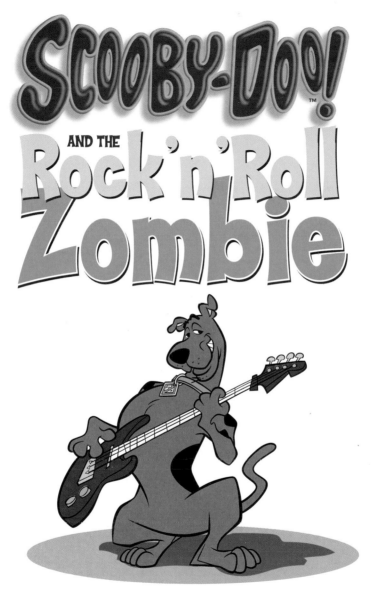

by Jesse Leon McCann

**visit us at www.abdopublishing.com**

Reinforced library bound edition published in 2010 by Spotlight, a division of the ABDO Group, 8000 West 78th Street, Edina, Minnesota 55439. Spotlight produces high-quality reinforced library bound editions for schools and libraries. Published by agreement with Warner Bros.—A Time Warner Company. The stories, characters, and incidents mentioned are entirely fictional. All rights reserved. Used under authorization.

Printed in the United States of America, Melrose Park, Illinois.
092009
012010

 PRINTED ON RECYCLED PAPER

Special thanks to Duendes del Sur for cover and interior illustrations.

**Library of Congress Cataloging-in-Publicatation**

McCann, Jesse Leon.
  Scooby-Doo and the rock 'n' roll zombie / by Jesse Leon McCann ; [illustrated by Duendes del Sur]. -- Reinforced library bound ed.
    p. cm.
  ISBN 978-1-59961-678-0
  I. Duendes Del Sur (Firm) II. Scooby-Doo (Television program) III. Title. IV. Title: Scooby-Doo and the rock and roll zombie.
  PZ7.M47835Scm 2010
  [Fic]--dc22

2009031240

All Spotlight books are reinforced library binding and manufactured in the United States of America.

Scooby-Doo and his pals from Mystery, Inc. went to a concert to see their favorite rock band, the Electric Pickle. Shaggy and Scooby loved the concert arena, especially the snack booths!

TICKETS

PIZZA

Daphne and Velma loved to dance to the beat. Fred loved the band's groovy tunes. Scooby and Shaggy thought the Electric Pickle played great music to eat by!

"Jeepers, there sure is a lot of fog!" Daphne said. "I wonder how Steve Stringbean, the lead singer, can see anything?"
Suddenly, as the fog cleared, there was a nasty surprise!

"Zoinks, it's a zombie!" Shaggy cried. "Like, it looks like there's a new lead singer!"

"A r-rombie?" Scooby gulped.

"There are no such things as zombies," Velma said.

The zombie started to sing: "I'm the Rock 'n' Roll Zombie, oh yeah, yeah! I'll bite your nose, and nibble on your toes!"

7

*"Huuurgh!"* the Rock 'n' Roll Zombie roared.

"Come on, gang!" said Fred. "We've got to stop that zombie. He's kidnapping Steve Stringbean!" As usual, Scooby and Shaggy didn't want to go along.

"We've searched everywhere, and there's no sign of them," Velma said.

Fred smiled, "Well, gang, looks like we have another mystery on our hands."

"Aww! Scoob and I were afraid you were going to say that!" Shaggy said.

The Mystery, Inc. kids looked for suspects and clues.
"It's a catastrophe! A crime!" said Nigel Moneybucks, the
band's manager. "Then again, it makes for great publicity!"

The gang split up to look for the zombie and Steve Stringbean. Fred, Daphne, and Velma checked Steve Stringbean's dressing room.

"Jinkies, look at this!" Velma said. "Somebody sure uses a lot of makeup!"

Meanwhile in the light booth, Shaggy and Scooby were in luck. *Bad* luck, that is!

The Rock 'n' Roll Zombie jumped out of an electrical closet! "*Arrrgh!*" it growled.

"Like, come on, Scoob!" Shaggy cried.

"*Roooh!*" Scooby-Doo didn't really want to go that way. He was afraid of heights!

The zombie sang as he chased them: "Oh yeah! You can run and you can hide! But in the end, I'm gonna make you cry-yi-yi!"

While Scooby and Shaggy were getting chased, the rest of the gang were interviewing suspects.

"If you ask me, he deserves getting kidnapped," said Molly Twigg, Steve Stringbean's ex-girlfriend. "He dumped me!"

Velma thought Molly or Nigel Moneybucks might be behind the mystery. Or maybe it was former band member Motley Mange.

"Yeah, he kicked me out of the Pickle!" Motley said. "We was mates!"

Just then, Scooby and Shaggy made a dramatic re-entrance.
They had lost the Rock 'n' Roll Zombie!
"*Hmm!* This gives me an idea!" Fred said.

"We have replaced Steve Stringbean with two new lead singers!" Daphne announced. "Please welcome back the Electric Pickle . . . with Shaggy and Scooby-Doo!"

Shaggy sang: "Like, monsters chase us all the time, man! Zoinks! We run as fast as we can, man!"
Scooby sang back-up harmony: "Roh-roh-roh!"

The Rock 'n' Roll Zombie didn't like Shaggy and Scooby's singing one bit!

"*Rrrrargh!*" it roared, as it came for them.

Fred and Velma were ready for the zombie's attack. Quick as a wink, the zombie was captured! Fred's plan had worked!

"Just as I thought! These crooked security guards were behind the Rock 'n' Roll Zombie mystery!" Velma said. "Only they had keys to the dressing rooms, where they stashed the zombie makeup kit."

Steve Stringbean was found safe, tied-up in the basement. The security guards planned to hold him for ransom.

"We would have gotten away with it, too, if it weren't for you meddling kids and your dog!" grumbled one of the security guards.

The Electric Pickle concert came back on, and they rocked! They even invited the Mystery, Inc. gang to join them on the stage, with Shaggy and Scooby-Doo as back-up singers! "Roh-yeah-yeah! Scooby-dooby-doo!"